DATE DUE		
AUG 0 8 2006		
OCT 0 7 2006		

201-9500   PRINTED IN U.S.A.

A Dog Named SAM

Janice Boland
pictures by G. Brian Karas

Dial Books for Young Readers • *New York*

Published by Dial Books for Young Readers
A Division of Penguin Books USA Inc.
375 Hudson Street
New York, New York 10014

The Dial Easy-to-Read logo is a registered trademark of
Dial Books for Young Readers,
a division of Penguin Books USA Inc.,
® TM 1,162,718.

First Edition
1 3 5 7 9 10 8 6 4 2

Library of Congress Cataloging in Publication Data
Boland, Janice.
A dog named Sam / by Janice Boland; pictures by G. Brian Karas.
—1st ed. p. cm.
Summary: A dog named Sam fetches the wrong things,
swims in the wrong places, and keeps everyone
in the house awake when he can't go to sleep at night.
ISBN 0-8037-1530-7—ISBN 0-8037-1531-5 (library)
[1. Dogs—Fiction.] I. Karas, G. Brian, ill. II. Title.
PZ7.B635849Do 1996 [E]—dc20 94-41554 CIP AC

The full-color artwork was prepared using gouache, acrylic, and pencil.
It was then color-separated and reproduced as red, blue, yellow, and black halftones.

Reading Level 1.8

To my sons Robert and John,
and for my father and our dog, Max
J.B.

CONTENTS

FETCH, SAM

Sam

Sam loved to fetch.

He loved it more than barking.

He loved it more than chewing.

He loved it more than digging holes

in the ground.

In the morning
Sam fetched every sock
in the drawer for Noah.
"Good dog, Sam!" said Noah.

Sam fetched all the shoes
in the closet for Molly.
"Thanks, Sam," said Molly.

Sam walked Molly and Noah
to the bus stop.

On the way he fetched balls.

He fetched sticks.

He fetched everything that
he could fit into his mouth.

The school bus came.

Molly and Noah got on.

Sam was left behind.

He had to fetch something....

THUNK!

Sam heard the newspaper

land on the porch.

He fetched it.

"What a good dog!" said Father.

He patted Sam's head and left for work.

And Sam fetched every newspaper

from every porch on the block.

"No, Sam!" said Mother.

She had to return every newspaper

to every porch on the block.

Mother was not happy.

While Mother was gone,

Sam saw socks hanging

on the clothesline next door.

They looked like Noah's socks.

Sam fetched them.

When Mother came back,

Sam had fetched the whole clothesline.

"Oh Sam, what shall I do with you?"

said Mother.

She had to put back the clothesline

and all of the clothes.

"No more fetching," said Mother.

Sam climbed up on Noah's bed.

He put his chin on his paws.

He had to fetch *something*.

Sam heard the school bus.

Now he knew what he had to fetch!

Sam rushed down the stairs.

He ran to the door.

Mother opened it wide.

Sam flew out of the house.

He raced to the bus stop.

And he fetched Molly and Noah.

Sam loved to fetch!

GET OUT

OF THE WATER, SAM

Sam liked water. He was made for it.

His tail was flat.

His toes were webbed.

His fur was thick and tight.

Whenever Sam saw water, he jumped in.

19

Sam followed Molly and Noah

to the beach.

He leaped into the water.

"Get out of the water!"

shouted the lifeguard.

"No dogs allowed!"

Sam went fishing with Father.

He jumped into the lake.

"Get out of the water!"

cried all of the other fishermen.

"You're scaring the fish!"

Mother took Sam to the park.

He lay down in a fountain.

"Get out of the water!"

yelled a policeman.

He pulled Sam out of the fountain.

And he sent him home with Mother.

23

But nothing stopped Sam.

He soaked in puddles.

He climbed into bathtubs.

He sat down in sinks.

Wherever he went, Sam heard,

"Get out of the water, Sam!"

One hot sunny day Sam heard splashing.

He heard laughing.

There was a pool party going on.

And the pool was full of water!

Sam ran through the crowd

and jumped into the water.

"There's a dog in the pool!"

shouted the boys and the girls.

"It's Sam!" cried Molly and Noah.

Everyone jumped into the pool.

They wanted to be in the water with Sam.

27

Sam floated. Sam splashed.

Sam slid down the slide.

And no one yelled,

"Get out of the water, Sam!"

GOOD NIGHT, SAM

It was bedtime.

"Good night, Sam," said Molly and Noah.

"Good night, Sam," said Mother and Father.

Then they all went upstairs to bed.

Sam was alone downstairs.

And he was wide awake.

He emptied his toy box.

He chewed his rubber bone.

He tossed his ball around.

Soon Sam had nothing left to do.

Sam looked out the window.

The moon was bright.

It was a good time to sing.

Sam threw back his head and sang.

"Sam, stop that noise!" called Mother.

"We're trying to sleep."

Sam stopped singing.

And everyone upstairs went back to sleep.

Suddenly Sam heard MONSTERS

in the garbage!

He smelled ROBBERS in the garden!

It was a good time to bark.

Sam barked and barked and BARKED!

"Quiet, Sam!" shouted Father.

"Go to sleep!"

Sam stopped barking.

And everyone upstairs

went back to sleep. Again.

Sam sniffed the night air.

It was a good time for a walk.

Sam scratched at the doors.

Scratch, scratch, scratch.

"Stop that scratching!"

yelled Molly, Noah, Mother, and Father.

Sam lay down. He looked around.

The TV was off. The chairs were empty.

The house was big and dark.

It was a good time to whimper.

It was a good time to whine.

It was a good time to HOWL!

Sam's howls filled the house.

Mother and Father covered their ears.

Molly and Noah buried their heads
under their pillows.

But they could not go back to sleep.

"It's almost morning," moaned Father.

"We might as well get up," groaned Mother.

Everyone put on their clothes.

Then they all went downstairs.

"Fetch your leash, Sam," said Molly.

"It's time for a walk," said Noah.

Sam lay down and closed his eyes.

He was tired. He had had a busy night.

It was a good time to sleep.

Good night, Sam.

TCR